TO SARA AND HANA CEPIĆ

AND LOVE TO MONIKA AND LUKA, MY TWO BIG BOUNCERS

HODDER CHILDREN'S BOOKS

First published in Great Britain in 2013
by Hodder and Stoughton

This paperback edition published in 2017

Text and illustrations copyright © David Melling, 2013

The moral rights of the author have been asserted.

A CIP catalogue record for this book
is available from the British Library.

ISBN: 978 1 444 94905 6

10 9 8 7 6 5 4 3 2 1

Printed and bound in China

FSC
www.fsc.org
MIX
Paper from
responsible sources
FSC® C104740

Hodder Children's Books
An imprint of Hachette Children's Group
Part of Hodder and Stoughton
Carmelite House
50 Victoria Embankment
London EC4Y 0DZ
An Hachette UK Company

www.hachette.co.uk
www.hachettechildrens.co.uk

www.davidmelling.co.uk

www.huglessdouglas.co.uk

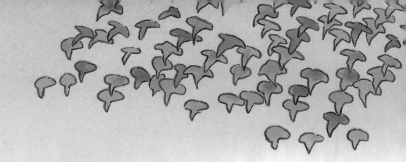

WE LOVE YOU, HUGLESS DOUGLAS

David Melling

Hodder Children's Books

It was a bright and beautiful kind of day.

'A day for sharing with friends,' thought Douglas.

So he went out to look for someone to play with.

Only he couldn't find anyone.

Anywhere.

Until he heard a noise…

'Hello Flossie,' said Douglas. 'How did you get up there?'

Flossie took a deep breath. 'I was playing hide-and-seek with **MY BEST FRIEND LITTLE SHEEP** and I got stuck and now he's lost and…'

'Don't worry,' said Douglas. And he placed Flossie gently on the ground.

Flossie gave Douglas a **THANK YOU HUG!**

'Please will you help me find Little Sheep?'
she sniffed.
'Of course I will,' said Douglas.

And together they headed off to do just that.

They soon passed the Old Barn and found Cow
and her best friend preparing frothy-top milkshakes
for everyone.

'Hellooo,' said Cow. 'Take a seat and we'll make you strawberry and banana smooOOOoo-thies!'

'We can't stop now, Cow,' said Douglas.
'We're looking for Little Sheep. Have you seen him?'

Cow looked under the table. 'Nooooo!' she said.
'Have you tried going down, through and round about?'

Douglas wasn't quite
sure what she meant but
thanked her all the same
and hurried on.

Douglas and Flossie made their way down the hill,
through the long, tickly grass towards Tall Tree Wood.

They were busy searching
around and about when
all of a sudden they were
surprised by three Funny
Bunnies!

'Good catch!' said Rabbit. 'Have you come to join our class, **BEST FRIEND BOUNCERS?**'
'No,' said Douglas. 'We're looking for Little Sheep.'

'Pity, I could do with a catcher for my big bouncers,'
Rabbit sighed. 'Well, if you're looking for sheep,
why don't you try Baa Baa Bush?'

By the time they reached Baa Baa Bush, Flossie
was very excited.
'Let's see what we can find in here,' said Douglas
and he rummaged around in the leaves.

There was no sign of any sheep. But Flossie wriggled and squeaked and asked Douglas to look again…

'Found you, Little Sheep!'
cried Flossie.

'BEST FRIENDS TOGETHER AT LAST,'
smiled Douglas.

The two sheep looked so happy and trotted off hand in hand.

Douglas waved them goodbye.
'I WISH *I* HAD A BEST FRIEND,'
he said.

Close by,
wise old Owl
heard his wish.

Douglas wondered why he felt so sad and sat down to think for a while.

He was just about to head home when he heard
a rustling sound behind him…

Everyone was there!

'We heard you needed a best friend,' said Rabbit.
'So we all came to find you.'

They were busy searching around and about when all of a sudden they were surprised by three Funny Bunnies!

'Good catch!' said Rabbit. 'Have you come to join our class, **BEST FRIEND BOUNCERS?**'

'No,' said Douglas. 'We're looking for Little Sheep.'

'Pity, I could do with a catcher for my big bouncers,'
Rabbit sighed. 'Well, if you're looking for sheep,
why don't you try Baa Baa Bush?'

By the time they reached Baa Baa Bush, Flossie
was very excited.
'Let's see what we can find in here,' said Douglas
and he rummaged around in the leaves.

There was no sign of any sheep. But Flossie wriggled and squeaked and asked Douglas to look again…

'Found you, Little Sheep!'
cried Flossie.

'BEST FRIENDS TOGETHER AT LAST,'
smiled Douglas.

The two sheep looked so happy and trotted off hand in hand.

Douglas waved them goodbye.
'I WISH *I* HAD A BEST FRIEND,'
he said.

Close by,
wise old Owl
heard his wish.

Douglas wondered why he felt so sad and sat down
to think for a while.

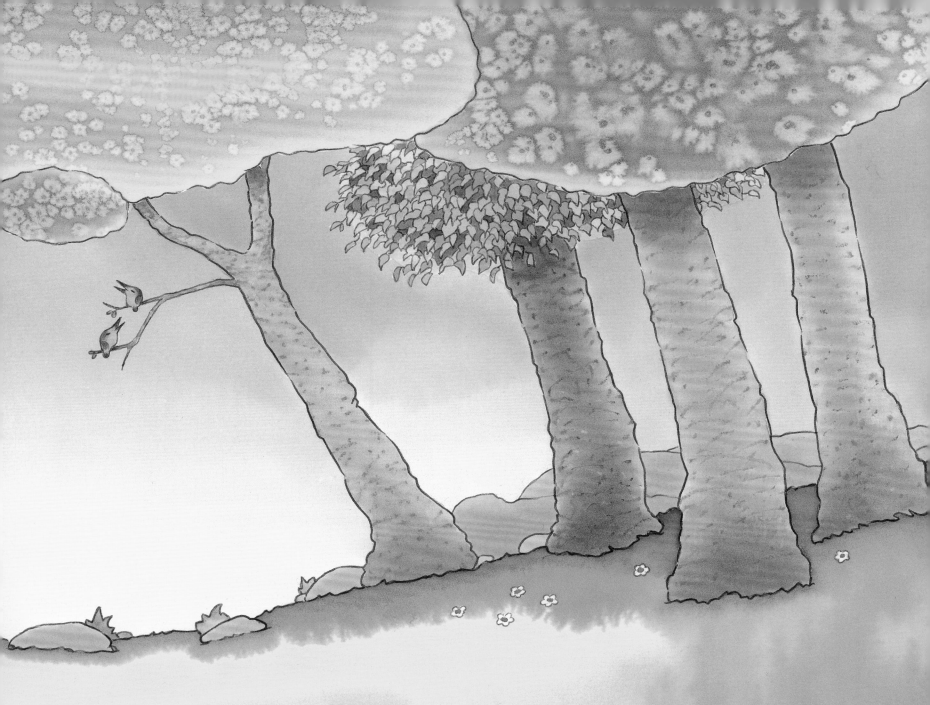

He was just about to head home when he heard
a rustling sound behind him…

Everyone was there!

'We heard you needed a best friend,' said Rabbit.
'So we all came to find you.'

Douglas realised how silly he had been.
'Of course, we're ALL best friends together.'

'WE LOVE YOU, HUGLESS DOUGLAS!'
everyone cried.
'And I love you too,' smiled Douglas.

I ♥ badges

We ♥ piggybacks

I ♥ muddy puddles

I ♥ drawing and painting

I ♥ ladybirds

I ♥ my mum

We ♥ bouncing

I ♥ my best friend

I ♥ pudding

I ♥ books

I ♥ my dad

HEART-SHAPED BISCUITS
YOU WILL NEED...

FOR THE BISCUITS:
- A lined or lightly greased baking sheet
- A mixing bowl
- A heart-shaped biscuit cutter

- 225g plain flour
- 75g caster sugar
- 150g butter
- Half a teaspoon of vanilla extract

FOR THE DECORATION:
- Some icing sugar
- Sprinkles and sweets
- Writing icing

1. Ask a grown-up to turn on the oven to 190°C/170°C fan/gas mark 5

2. **CUT** the butter into small squares, then add the sugar and flour into a mixing bowl

3. **RUB** all the ingredients together to make a dough

4. **SHAPE** the dough into a ball, wrap it in cling film and put it in the fridge to chill for 10 minutes

5. **ROLL** the dough out on a floured surface until it is about half a centimetre thick, then cut out your biscuits using your cutter and lay them on the baking sheet

6. **BAKE** for 15 minutes or until the biscuits are golden brown

7. Ask a grown-up to take the biscuits out of the oven and place them on a wire rack to cool

8. When the biscuits are cool, **MIX** the icing sugar with a little warm water and spread on top

9. Now **DECORATE** with the writing icing, sprinkles and sweets. You could try drawing hearts with red icing or writing the name of your best friend on the biscuit